Hamish finds Himself

First published 2005
Evans Brothers Limited
2A Portman Mansions
Chiltern St
London W1U 6NR

British Library Cataloguing in Publication Data
Powell, Jillian
    Hamish finds himself. – (Zig zag)
    1. Children's stories – Pictorial works
    I. Title
    823.9'14 [J]

ISBN 0237529475
13-digit ISBN (from 1 January 2007) 9780237529475

Printed in China by WKT Company Ltd

Series Editor: Nick Turpin
Design: Robert Walster
Production: Jenny Mulvanny
Series Consultant: Gill Matthews

Hamish Finds Himself

by Jillian Powell

illustrated by Belinda Worsley

Evans

Hamish was the youngest in his family.

Sometimes that was fun.

But it wasn't always fair.
Hamish never had anything new.
He always had old things.

He had Ben's old computer.

He had Tom's old bike.

He even had Ben's old bed,
when Ben grew too big for it.

"It's not fair," Hamish said. "I never have anything that is just mine!"

So he went out to find something that was just his.

First, he found a feather.

But the feather belonged to a bird.

Then he found a shell.

But the shell belonged to
a snail.

Then, he found a ball.

But the ball belonged to
a dog first.

"I'll never find anything that is just mine!" Hamish said.

Then Hamish saw something.

26

He did a handstand.
Then he did
a cartwheel.

Hamish had found something
that was just his!

Why not try reading another ZigZag book?

Dinosaur Planet	ISBN: 0 237 52667 0
by David Orme and Fabiano Fiorin	
Tall Tilly	ISBN: 0 237 52668 9
by Jillian Powell and Tim Archbold	
Batty Betty's Spells	ISBN: 0 237 52669 7
by Hilary Robinson and Belinda Worsley	
The Thirsty Moose	ISBN: 0 237 52666 2
by David Orme and Mike Gordon	
The Clumsy Cow	ISBN: 0 237 52656 5
by Julia Moffatt and Lisa Williams	
Open Wide!	ISBN: 0 237 52657 3
by Julia Moffatt and Anni Axworthy	
Too Small	ISBN 0 237 52777 4
by Kay Woodward and Deborah van de Leijgraaf	
I Wish I Was An Alien	ISBN 0 237 52776 6
by Vivian French and Lisa Williams	
The Disappearing Cheese	ISBN 0 237 52775 8
by Paul Harrison and Ruth Rivers	
Terry the Flying Turtle	ISBN 0 237 52774 X
by Anna Wilson and Mike Gordon	
Pet To School Day	ISBN 0 237 52773 1
by Hilary Robinson and Tim Archbold	
The Cat in the Coat	ISBN 0 237 52772 3
by Vivian French and Alison Bartlett	
Pig in Love	ISBN 0 237 52950 5
by Vivian French and Tim Archbold	
The Donkey That Was Too Fast	ISBN 0 237 52949 1
by David Orme and Ruth Rivers	
The Yellow Balloon	ISBN 0 237 52948 3
by Helen Bird and Simona Dimitri	
Hamish Finds Himself	ISBN 0 237 52947 5
by Jillian Powell and Belinda Worsley	
Flying South	ISBN 0 237 52946 7
by Alan Durant and Kath Lucas	
Croc by the Rock	ISBN 0 237 52945 9
by Hilary Robinson and Mike Gordon	